Russ T. Hammer

To order additional copies of this book, contact:

Xlibris

844-714-8691

www.Xlibris.com

Orders@Xlibris.com

ISBN: Softcover   978-1-6698-0494-9

      EBook   978-1-6698-0493-2

Print information available on the last page

Rev. date: 03/11/2022

This book is dedicated to survivors of abuse and to his Dad, a World War II Veteran of Omaha Beach, who grew up with out a mother. John B. F. "The Major."

<u>A true American Hero.</u>

Believing, "Life is too short to be serious all the time, we need to laugh"

BOB IS SO HAPPY, HE FINALLY GOT
HIS Ph D.

HIS PRETTY huge DOG!

BOB DISCOVERS THE CREATURES WITH THE BLACK BALLOONS!

BOB VISITS "THE GRAPE PYRAMIDS," BUT CONFUSES THE SPHINX FOR HIS PRETTY HUGE DOG.

BOB GOT A PET MANATEE AND NAMED
HIM HUGH,
BOB FEEDS HIM EVERY DAY. THUS,
BOB'S CONTRIBUTION TO
"HUGH MANATEE!"

BOB VISITS A.G.T., BUT GETS ATTACKED BY THE GOLDEN BUZZARD!

BOB ON EASTER ISLAND POINTS OUT,
"THERE'S ALWAYS A FEW DRINKERS IN
EVERY FAMILY..."

When's our Tee Time?

No Bob, Ah... we're having a
Tea Party.

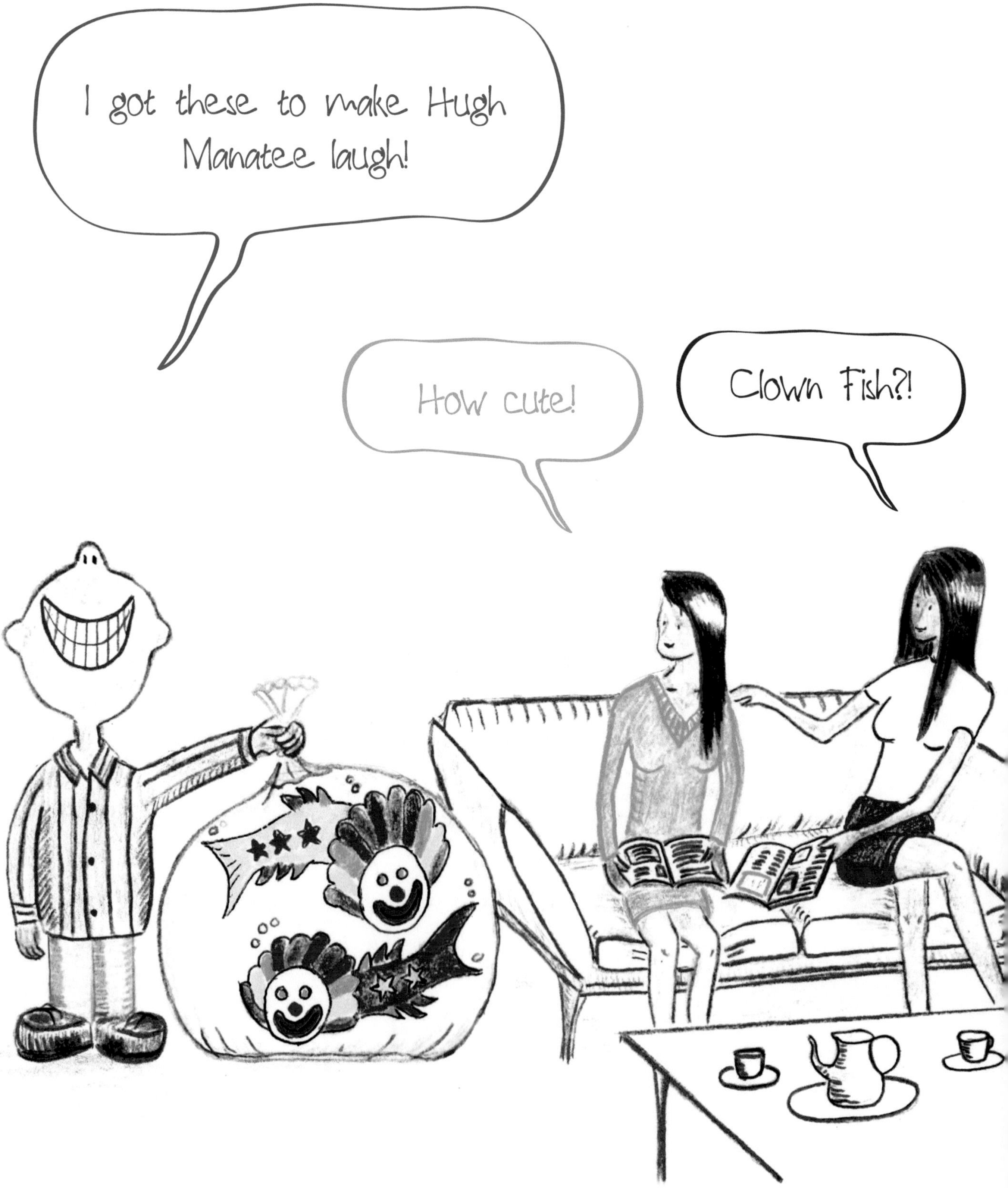
I got these to make Hugh Manatee laugh!
How cute!
Clown Fish?!

My brother might join
the Navy...

Gee Scooter, he should take
Pre-Naval Vitamins.

Crystal Gayle...

O.M.G. Bob wouldn't eat doughnut
because of that song!

Oh yah...
"Doughnuts make my brown eyes,
Doughnuts make my brown eyes,
Doughnuts make my brown eyes blue..."

14

In 1974, RUBIC replaced
Havana as the Capital

What do you mean?

Yah, haven't you heard of
"RUBICS CUBA?"

Can you take me to the Mall?
I need to get an Uncle Ranch...

What's an Uncle Ranch?

Well, I already have an Ant Farm
And we should take care of our
Relatives!

I worry...

About what?

Where does the Giant Weather Lady
Live?

Okay Mr. Bob...
put your arms out, bend for word, stand on one foot, and recite the Alphabet back-words!
Y-O-U- G-O-T- B-E- K-I-D-D-I-N-G- R-E-A-L-L-Y?!
BIKE TO WORK DAY
BIKE TO WORK DAY
NO BIKES ON THE MALL

Shhhh... Don't scare it, It's a very rare
Can-Koon...
I think you're from Mexico...?

He's beautiful to look at, but Bob's Lion-fish
Never tells the truth!

The Doctor told Bob,
"Give them a week and they'll become extinct,
Because
They're only Dino-sores..."

Bob got a Helper Dog.

What's he need a Helper Dog for?

It helps him pick-out his clothes.

That explains SO much!